PICKLE
PUSS

Books you will enjoy:

The Polka Dot Private Eye books:

THE MYSTERY OF THE BLUE RING
THE RIDDLE OF THE RED PURSE
THE SECRET AT THE POLK STREET SCHOOL
THE POWDER PUFF PUZZLE
THE CASE OF THE COOL-ITCH KID
GARBAGE JUICE FOR BREAKFAST
THE TRAIL OF THE SCREAMING TEENAGER
THE CLUE AT THE ZOO

YEARLING BOOKS are designed especially to entertain and enlighten young people. Patricia Reilly Giff, consultant to this series, received her bachelor's degree from Marymount College and a master's degree in history from St. John's University. She holds a Professional Diploma in Reading and a Doctorate of Humane Letters from Hofstra University. She was a teacher and reading consultant for many years, and is the author of numerous books for young readers.

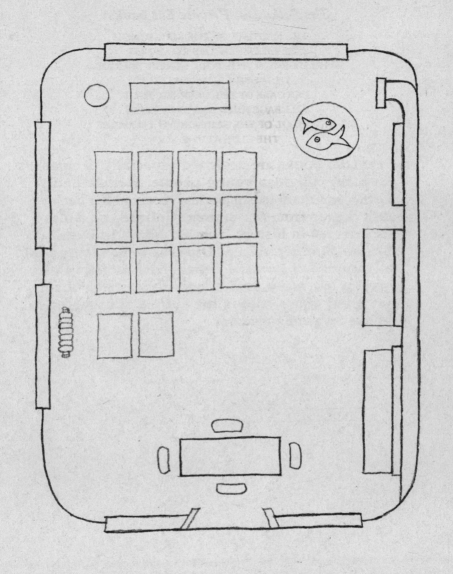

The Kids of the
12
Polk Street School

PICKLE
PUSS

Patricia Reilly Giff

Illustrated by Blanche Sims

A YEARLING BOOK

Published by
Bantam Doubleday Dell Books for Young Readers
a division of
Bantam Doubleday Dell Publishing Group, Inc.
1540 Broadway
New York, New York 10036

ISBN: 0-440-46844-2

Printed in the United States of America

August 1986

31 30

OPM

For Terri and Ed Reilly,
Freddie Schonenberg,
and
Lorne Norton
with love

Chapter 1

Emily Arrow jumped down the steps. She rushed across the lawn.

"Wait for me," her little sister, Stacy, yelled.

Emily looked back.

Stacy opened the screen door.

She was wearing a tablecloth on her head.

She had her mother's high heels on her feet.

"You can't go like that," Emily said.

"I'll take off my veil," Stacy said. She dropped the tablecloth. It landed on the grass.

Emily closed her eyes. "Hurry."

Stacy clicked down the path. "Mrs. Baker will love my red shoes."

Emily started across the street.

"Walk slow," Stacy said. "It's hard to keep up."

Emily took Stacy's hand. "Try. We're almost late."

At the next corner they saw Richard Best.

He was crawling under a bush.

"Hey, Beast," Emily called.

"Where are you going?" he yelled.

"To the library," Emily said. "Today's the day Fish for a Good Book starts. We can do it all month."

"Not me," Beast said. "I read enough in summer school. Too much." He sat back. "Besides, it's August. School starts soon."

"Emily's going to fish," Stacy said. "Right, Emily?"

Emily nodded. "I'm going to get a pile of them."

"So is Dawn," said Beast. "And Jill. And Timothy Barbiero." He shook his head. "Too bad Matthew moved away. He'd like to fish too."

"Did you hear from him?" Emily asked.

Beast held up one finger. "I got a letter. A skinny little letter. Matthew's a terrible speller. I couldn't understand it."

"Come on, Emily," Stacy said. "It's too hot to stand still."

Emily and Stacy went down the street. They turned in at the library.

"Whew," said Stacy. "Lots of kids are here today."

Emily waved at Jill and Dawn.

Then she looked up. There was a new picture on the wall.

It was a picture of a boy fishing. He was fishing in blue paper water.

Red and blue and tan paper fish swam in the water.

Up on top it said FISH FOR A GOOD BOOK.

"I'm going to get lots of fish," Stacy said.

Emily shook her head. "You don't have a card."

"Mrs. Baker will give me one," Stacy said.

"No," said Emily. "Not until you can write your name. That's the rule."

Stacy stuck her lip out. She looked as if she were going to cry. "How can I learn to write? Nobody will let me go to school."

Emily patted her shoulder. "Next year."

Just then Mrs. Baker came over. She smiled at them.

All her freckles crinkled up.

"I'm going to find a book," Emily told her. "A good one."

"Right," said Mrs. Baker. "I'll print your name on the chart. Then every time you read a book, you'll get a fish. You can put it next to your name.''

Emily went to the shelves. She pulled out a book. *Five Children and It.*

It was too fat.

''I read that book,'' said a boy.

Emily looked at him. He had a nice face.

He was the fifth-grade monitor in school.

''My name is Freddie S.,'' he told her. ''That's a good book.''

Emily looked down at the book.

It had about a skillion pages.

It would take forever to read.

''Well . . .'' she said.

''Go ahead. Try it,'' said Freddie.

''I guess so,'' Emily said.

She went to Mrs. Baker's desk.

Too bad she didn't have a skinnier book.

She looked back.

Freddie was talking with his friend Edward.

Emily stuck the fat book on the book cart.

She grabbed another one.

It was much skinnier.

She gave it to Mrs. Baker.

Mrs. Baker checked it out. "You like snakes?" she asked.

"Yucks," said Emily. Then she looked at the book.

There was a snake on the cover. It was the kind with the fat neck. Its tooth was sticking out.

"I mean, I love them," Emily said.

She grabbed the book.

She went out the door with Stacy.

Chapter 2

It was after supper the next week. Thursday.
Emily could hear the kids outside.

She looked down at her book. She was up to
page two. It was about cobras, snakes that lived
in India.

It said that cobras liked to spit. Sometimes
they spit in people's eyes.

It said some other things too.

Emily didn't know the words though.

She closed the book. She went outside.

"Hurry," Beast yelled. "It's almost dark."

"You're it," Dawn said.

Emily pressed her nose against the tree. She shut her eyes tight.

She loved to play hide-and-seek.

"Ten. Twenty. Thirty. Forty. Fifty," she yelled. "Here I come, ready or not."

"Not ready," Jill Simon shouted.

Emily waited a minute. She kept her eyes shut.

Jill was too fat to run fast.

Someone was hiding in the bushes.

Emily could hear him moving around.

It was probably Beast.

Without thinking, Emily opened her eyes.

"No fair peeking," Dawn Bosco called.

Emily made a face. "I'm not a cheater."

She thought about Dawn Bosco.

Dawn had three bathing suits.

She had ladybug earrings.

Her middle name was Tiffanie.

Sometimes she was a big pain.

Emily waited another minute.

Then she yelled, "Here I come. Right now."

She walked down the driveway. She could see something pink behind the fence.

It was one of Jill's bows.

She didn't look at Jill.

Jill would cry if she were caught.

Emily walked backward toward the bushes. She made believe she was looking at the tree.

She'd catch Beast.

She dived into the bushes. "Got you," she yelled.

Something yowled.

Emily jumped back.

A black-and-white cat streaked past her. "Hey," Emily yelled.

Just then she heard steps behind her.

Running steps.

Emily twirled around.

Dawn was racing for the tree.

Emily raced for the tree too. She tried to run faster than Dawn.

At the tree they bumped heads.

"Got you," Emily yelled.

"Home free," Dawn shouted.

"No fair," Emily said. "I tagged you first."

"I'm not playing with cheaters," Dawn said. She made a fresh face.

Emily wanted to pop her right in the mouth.

Beast came out from the backyard. "What's going on?"

Jill came out too.

"I'm going home," Dawn said.

"Don't do that," Beast said. "We can't play with only three kids."

Emily's little sister, Stacy, jumped off the steps.

"I'll play," she said.

Emily looked at her.

Stacy had red all over her mouth.

Ketchup.

They had eaten hamburgers for supper.

"You can't count," Emily said in a low voice.

"I can so," said Stacy out loud. "One, two, four, eight, five."

Just then they heard a whistle.

It was Beast's father.

"Time to go home," Beast said.

Emily started back up her path. "Come on, Stacy."

"Make up with Dawn," said Beast.

Emily turned around. "Want to make up?"

"Maybe." Dawn said. "And maybe not."

Emily stared at Dawn.

Dawn still had a fresh face.

"Not," said Emily.

"I'm going to have a pile of fish," said Dawn. "You'll probably have none."

Emily stamped up her steps. "Watch out

for cobras," she said. "They'll spit in your eye."

"Pickle puss," said Dawn.

Emily stuck out her tongue.

She slammed into the house.

Chapter 3

Emily held her nose. She took a deep breath.
She jumped into her pool.
The water was cold.
Freezing.
She came to the top. "Yeow," she screeched.
She hung on to the side.

Her little sister, Stacy, looked up from her dirt pile. "Mommy said to turn on the hose in front."

"Do it for me," Emily begged.

Stacy shook her head. "Can't. The turner-on thing is too hard."

Emily sighed. She climbed out of the pool.

She ran down the driveway on tiptoes.

She had to watch out for sharp stones.

She looked up. Jill was coming toward her.

Jill had yellow bows on her braids today. Her bathing suit was yellow too.

She looked like a fat yellow beach ball.

"Hi, Emily," she said. "Can I go for a swim?"

"Sure. Go ahead," Emily said. She scooted around Jill.

She bent over and turned on the sprinkler.

Dawn Bosco passed by on the other side of the street.

"Hey, Dawn," she yelled.

Dawn didn't answer. She started to run.

Emily watched her.

Dawn had two books in her arms. One fell on the ground.

She stopped to pick it up. "I'll have a fish today," she yelled.

She turned the corner.

Emily made her neck fat. She jerked her head forward. "Right in the eye," she said.

She went back to the yard.

Jill was floating in the water. Her bows were floating too.

Stacy was pouring water on a pile of dirt. "Mud-mud-muddies," she sang.

"Don't talk to me," Emily said. "I'm going to read."

She sat down on the grass. She picked up her book.

She read the last five pages.

Snakes were pretty good, she thought. They had to watch out for mongooses though.

Emily looked at a picture of a mongoose.

It was a long,skinny thing with fur.

It looked a little like Dawn Bosco.

Emily closed her book. "I saw Dawn," she told Jill.

Jill gave a tiny kick. "Dawn's going to have a hundred fish."

"Dawn's a pickle puss," Emily said.

Stacy stuck her lip out. "Mommy said don't call people pickle pusses."

"Get lost, Stacy," Emily said.

"Mommy," Stacy screamed.

"Besides," Jill said. "Dawn called Emily a pickle puss too. Remember?"

"Snaggle doodles on Dawn," Emily said. "She's not going to beat me."

"Good," said Jill.

"Get out of the pool," Emily told her. "Let's go to the library."

Jill squeezed out her braids. Water dripped

off the ends. "I'll go home and get dressed."
She climbed out of the pool.

"I'm going to get a fish," Emily said. "I
finished my snake book. And I'm going to get
more books too. The skinniest minniest—"

"Can I come?" Stacy asked.

Emily frowned at her.

"All right," said Stacy. "Dawn's a pickle
puss. Dawn's a double pickle puss."

"Well . . ." Emily said.

Stacy slammed her pail on her dirt pile.

"Pan-pan-pancake," she sang. She stood up.
"I'm ready."

Emily rushed up to her bedroom.

She threw her bathing suit behind the bed.

She put on her shorts and her blue freckle-dot
shirt.

She could hear Stacy singing, "Going to the
li-li-li-berry."

Emily went downstairs again. She'd show Dawn Bosco.

If anybody had a hundred fish, it wouldn't be Dawn.

It would be Emily. Emily Arrow.

Chapter 4

Emily crossed the street.

Jill and Stacy walked right behind her.

Beast was kneeling under his tree.

Emily went closer. "What are you doing?"

Beast turned around. He had a cat in his arms. "Look what I found."

The cat was black. It had one white ear. It had a white tip on its tail.

"I saw him last week," Emily said.

The cat wiggled to get out of Beast's arms.

Beast put it down. "I found him in my tree."

Emily reached out to pet the cat.

The cat put its back up in the air. It took a dancing step.

"He's a brave one," Emily said. "That's the best kind."

Stacy began to sing. "Tough-tough-toughie."

The cat grabbed one of Emily's sneaker laces. It began to pull.

"What's his name?" Jill asked.

"Cat," said Beast. "I want to keep him." He raised his shoulders in the air. "But my mother said no."

"I'll take him." Emily crossed her fingers. "If my mother says."

"I'm feeding him," Beast said. "Milk and potato chips."

Jill tossed her braids in the air. "You can't give a cat potato chips."

"This cat likes them." Beast poured some out of the bag.

He licked his fingers. "I like them too."

"Let me hold him," Emily said. She picked up the cat.

It began to chew on her collar.

"He should have a nice name," Emily said. "A name like—"

"Blacky," Jill said.

"Tippy," said Beast.

Emily shook her head. "Maybe—"

"My turn," said Stacy. "Let me hold him now."

"Wait," Emily said.

"Come on, Emily." Stacy pulled on her arm.

"I'd take him," Jill said. "But I have a dog."

"Em-i-ly," Stacy said. "I want the cat right now."

"Don't squish him," Beast said.

"I won't," Stacy said. "What do you think—I'm a baby?"

Emily tickled the cat's chin.

She gave it to Stacy. "Just for a minute."

The cat licked Stacy's cheek. Then it pulled on her hair.

"Ouch," Stacy said. "Pickle Puss."

Just then Freddie passed by. "Nice cat," he said.

"He's Emily's," said Stacy. "Maybe."

"How's the book?" Freddic asked Emily. *"Five Children and It."*

Emily thought about the book. She remembered putting it on the cart.

She couldn't tell that to Freddie.

"It's very good," she said. She crossed her fingers.

"I knew you'd like it." Freddie crossed the street. "See you later."

"Give the cat back now," Beast told Stacy. "He wants potato chips. Nice salty ones."

Stacy shook her head.

Beast reached for the cat.

The cat jumped out of Stacy's arms.

It raced down the street.

Beast raced after it.

Emily started to run too.

"Get him," Stacy yelled. "Get my cat."

"What about the library?" Jill called.

Emily kept going.

She turned the corner.

She dashed up the street.

She had to get the cat.

Suppose he got lost again?

They might never find him.

Chapter 5

Emily wiped her face.

She was dirty. Filthy.

She had run all over the place. She had crawled under a dozen bushes.

The cat was gone.

"Poor, poor cat," said Stacy.

"No home," said Jill. "No food."

"Not even potato chips," said Stacy.

Emily felt a lump in her throat. "Sad," she said. "Maybe Beast will find him."

She opened the library door. "I'm going to buy cat food. Just in case we find him. I have my tooth money."

Inside, Emily looked at the FISH FOR A GOOD BOOK picture.

Then she looked at the chart.

Lots of kids had a fish next to their names.

Dawn had a red one.

Emily picked a tan fish. She tacked it next to her name.

It looked a little bigger than Dawn's red one.

Dawn Mongoose Bosco.

Stacy looked up at her. "I wish I had my name up there."

"Next year," Emily said.

"Too long," said Stacy. "And I don't even have a cat anymore."

Mrs. Baker went past. She patted Stacy on the head.

"Did you see a cat?" Stacy called after her.

"When did you lose it?" Mrs. Baker asked.

"Two minutes ago," Stacy said.

Mrs. Baker shook her head. "I'm sorry."

"He's this big," Stacy said.

She bent down.

She put her hand an inch above the floor.

"That's pretty small," said Mrs. Baker.

"Well, maybe a little bigger," Stacy said.

"A lot bigger," said Emily. She looked around.

She didn't see Dawn.

Dawn was probably home.

Reading as fast as she could.

"I'll get a book," Stacy said. "You can read it to me." She knelt down next to the picture books.

Emily went to a bookcase in back. She needed books fast.

Easy ones.

She pulled out two. She didn't even read the titles.

They were skinny minnies.

Books with lots of pictures.

She was glad Freddie wasn't around. She didn't want him to see them.

Stacy came over. She held up a book. "What's this?"

Emily looked at it. Her mother had read it to her when she was small. "It's called *Make Way for Ducklings.*"

"Very good," Stacy said.

They went to the desk.

"What's the prize?" Stacy asked Mrs. Baker. "The Fish for a Good Book prize?"

"The real prize is reading a good book," said Mrs. Baker.

"I like a real prize that's candy," said Stacy.

Mrs. Baker smiled. "We're going to have a party. It will be on the last day of the contest. You can come, Stacy."

Jill came up behind them. "I have a cat book."

"You have a cat too?" Mrs. Baker asked.

"Almost," Jill said.

Mrs. Baker crinkled up her freckles. "I love cats."

Emily pushed her books over.

Mrs. Baker looked at them. "Are you going to read to Stacy?"

"Only one," said Stacy. "The rest are Emily's."

Emily stared down at her sneakers.

Maybe Mrs. Baker thought she was a baby.

Maybe Mrs. Baker thought she just wanted fish.

Emily grabbed the books. "Let's go, Stacy."
She hurried out the door.

Chapter 6

Emily found the last strawberry in her cereal. She popped it into her mouth. It tasted wonderful.

She twisted the radio knob. The weatherman was saying it was hot.

He was right, Emily thought. She put the bowl in the sink.

Then she went out the door.

Beast was waiting. They wanted to find the cat today.

Stacy was outside too. She was wearing an old Halloween costume.

"I'm Stacy Arrow—Princess," Stacy said. "I'll come with you."

They went down the street.

They turned the corner.

"Here, kitty," Emily called.

"How do you make an *S*?" Stacy asked. "For my name."

"Like a snake," said Emily. She made her neck fat. She hissed a little.

"I know that one." Stacy began to screech: "Here, cat. Come to Stacy."

"You're going to scare him away," said Beast.

They looked under the bushes.

"*S* like a snake," Stacy sang. "A Stacy snake."

They passed Dawn Bosco's house.

Dawn was sitting on her front steps. She was reading a fat book.

"Snaggle doodles," Emily said.

"Hi, Dawn," Beast yelled. "Want to help us look for a cat?"

Dawn put her book down. "Sure," she said. "I have a cat now too. I found him."

Emily frowned a little. "What does he look like?"

"What comes next after *S*?" Stacy said.

"Never mind," Emily said. She looked at Dawn. "What—"

"Tell me," Stacy said. "Please."

Emily made a cross with her two thumbs. "*T*."

Stacy nodded. "I almost forgot."

Dawn bent down to look under a car.

Emily bent down to look too. "My cat is black and white," she said.

"Mine has a white tip on his tail," said Dawn.

"Hey," said Beast. "There he is."

Emily stood up. "Where?"

"Look." Beast pointed up. "In the tree."

Emily shaded her eyes.

"Here, Pickle Puss," Stacy yelled. "Come on down."

"I have cat food," Emily told Dawn.

"He's mine," said Dawn.

"I'll get him," Beast said.

He jumped for a branch.

The cat meowed.

"I saw him first," Emily said.

"My mother said I could have him," said Dawn.

"So did mine. I asked her last night," said Emily. "My mother was glad."

She crossed her fingers. Her mother hadn't been so glad. Emily had begged until her mother said yes.

Beast reached up. The cat climbed on his arm.

"Yeow," said Beast. "His claws are sharp."

He climbed down with it.

Emily grabbed for the cat.

So did Dawn.

"Wait," said Beast. "Choose for him."

"I'm not choosing," said Dawn.

"Me neither," said Emily.

"Want to make a bet?" asked Beast.

"He's really mine," said Dawn. "He slept with me last night."

"What bet?" Emily asked.

Beast looked up in the air. "Whoever gets the most fish keeps him."

Stacy frowned. "Emily's not such a hot reader."

"All right," said Dawn. "I'll bet."

"I am so a hot reader," said Emily. "I'll bet too."

"Cross your heart?" Dawn said. "Hope to die?"

"Spit on my toes," Emily said.

Beast put the cat down.

Emily reached for it.

So did Dawn.

Dawn scooped it up. "I'll keep him for now. He likes it at my house."

Emily stood there for another minute.

She wanted to grab the cat.

She put her nose up in the air. "Mongoose."

"What's that?" Dawn asked.

"Come on," Emily told Stacy. "I'm going home to read."

Chapter 7

Today was Friday. August was half over.

Emily sat on her front step. She looked up at the tree. She could hear a locust buzzing.

She held her two skinny-minny books on her lap.

No one else was around.

Jill was at the store with her mother. They were buying stuff for school.

Beast had to stay in today.

He had run his bike over his mother's daisies.

Even Stacy was staying overnight at Aunt Anne's.

Emily looked at one of the books.

It was a book on tying knots.

Emily knew how to tie knots.

It was silly to read a whole book about them.

She made her eyes cross.

The knots ran together.

She turned the pages as fast as she could.

Then she slapped the book shut.

She picked up the other one.

It had a picture of a tree on the front. A green tree.

She had read that one a long time ago. Maybe when she was in kindergarten.

No good. She'd have to bring it back to the library.

Mrs. Baker had said old books didn't count.

She stood up.

She didn't feel like walking four blocks.

It was no fun alone.

She'd try to hold her breath.

She'd see how many breaths it took to get there.

She breathed in as hard as she could.

She started to run.

A neighbor was standing on the corner. "Hi, Emily," Mrs. Mann said.

Emily let her breath out.

"Your face is red," Mrs. Mann said. "Are you sunburned?"

Emily nodded. She didn't want Mrs. Mann to know she was holding her breath.

She took another breath and started across the street.

It took her eleven breaths to get to the library.

On the way home she'd try to do it in ten.

Mrs. Baker wasn't at the desk.

There was another woman there. The library helper.

She took the two books from Emily. ''Help yourself to two fish,'' she said.

Emily opened her mouth.

The library helper pointed to the chart. ''Take any two you want. Put them next to your name.''

Emily went over to the chart. She looked at her tan fish.

Then she looked at Dawn's name.

Dawn had two fish now.

''Hey, Emily,'' a voice said.

It was Freddie.

His friend Edward was there too.

''Take a red fish,'' Edward told Emily.

Emily stood on one foot.

She picked a red fish and tacked it up.

''Don't forget the other fish,'' Edward said.

Emily stared at her name for a minute.

It was bad enough to take a fish for the knot book.

It had taken two minutes to read it.

But it was wrong to take one for the tree book.

"Go ahead," said Freddie. "Here."

He pulled off a blue fish. He tacked it next to her name.

Emily licked her lip. "Thanks," she said.

She went to get another book.

She picked out an in-between kind.

Not a fat one.

Not a skinny minny.

She wasn't going to read skinny minnies anymore.

It wasn't fair.

On the way home she breathed in hard.

Then she let her breath out.

She didn't want to play holding breaths anymore.

At least she had more fish than Dawn now.

She didn't feel better though.

If only Freddie hadn't put up the blue fish.
Maybe she should have stopped him.
She went up her front porch.
She wanted to cry.

Chapter 8

A blue fish was swimming after Emily.

It was going to grab her.

Emily tried to swim faster.

Then she felt the sun on her face.

She was in her own bed.

She opened one eye.

She didn't want to think about the blue fish.

Maybe she'd think about her new book. The in-between one.

It was all about a girl. A funny girl like Stacy. Her name was Ramona.

She had read a pile of pages last night.

Today she'd read another pile.

"Wake up, Emily," Stacy said. "I want to show you something."

Emily opened her other eye.

Stacy waved a paper around.

"What's that?" Emily asked. She looked at a bunch of scribble-scrabble lines.

"Can't you tell?" Stacy asked.

"Is it a picture of a railroad track?"

Stacy shook her head.

"I give up," Emily said.

Stacy leaned over her. "It's a Stacy. Part of a Stacy."

Emily turned the paper upside down.

She could see a big shaky S.

She could almost see a t.

"*S* for Stacy Snake," said Stacy. "And the crossing-thumbs one. *T*."

"Not bad," Emily said. "Too big though."

"I like them big," said Stacy. "I like to see them."

Emily reached for her book.

Stacy leaned closer. "I wish I could write my name. I wish it more than anything."

Emily sat up.

"I want to get a card," Stacy said.

She tapped on Emily's foot.

"I don't care about my name on the wall." Tap.

"I don't care about a fish." Tap.

"I want to get my own books myself." Tap.

Emily blinked. "I won't have a foot left."

"Sorry," Stacy said.

Emily looked down at her book. "I have to read," she told Stacy. "August is almost over."

Dawn was probably reading too.

Maybe she'd catch up with Emily. Maybe she'd even pass her.

Emily looked up.

Stacy had milk around her mouth.

Her brown eyes had tears in them.

Emily sighed. "Get me some paper," she said. "Get a whole bunch."

Stacy jumped off the bed. "What are we going to do?"

"We're going to write your name," Emily said. "A hundred times. Until you know it."

Stacy went down the hall. "Hundred-nun-dred," she sang.

Emily slid out of bed.

She put on her torn pink shorts.

She put on her I HATE SPINACH shirt.

She looked under the bed for her flip-flops.

"Here I am," Stacy said. "Ready or not."

51

Emily sat on the floor. She put on her flip-flops. "Make an *S*. Make a *t*."

She leaned over Stacy. "Not so big."

Stacy made an *S*. She made a little *t*. "Look at that skinny little thing. Small as anything," she said.

Emily looked at it. "Make another one. Make it darker."

Stacy put her tongue out a little. She wrote another *S-t*. "Perfect," she said.

"Almost," said Emily. "Now we're going to do an *a*."

She drew one for Stacy on the paper.

"*A* has a nice fat stomach," said Stacy, singing. She leaned over the paper.

Emily swallowed. Stacy's *a* was terrible.

She'd have to do it over and over.

They'd be sitting on the floor all morning.

All day. All week.

"You're a good-good-sister," Stacy sang. She wiped her mouth on her hand.

Emily smiled.

She tried not to think about Dawn.

"I know," she said.

Chapter 9

It was Thursday again. School would begin next week.

Today was the last day to fish for a good book. Tomorrow was the library party.

Emily sat in the driveway reading.

Stacy sat next to her. She had a purple crayon. She was writing *y*'s.

They looked like *4*'s.

"Two pages to go," Emily said. "I love this book."

She took the crayon.

She made a *y* with nice arms.

"Very pretty," Stacy said. "I can do that too."

Emily turned the page of her book.

She'd have four fish today.

She'd take another tan one.

Too bad she kept thinking about that blue fish.

She bit her thumbnail.

She should have three fish.

Not four.

"Only babies suck their thumbs," Stacy said.

"Snaggle doodles," said Emily. She looked up.

Beast and Jill and Dawn were coming down the street.

Pickle Puss was curled around Dawn's neck.

"You have a fur coat," Stacy yelled.

"Want to play something?" Beast asked.

The three of them came up the path.

Emily reached out.

She gave the cat a pat.

It yanked on Dawn's hair.

"Crazy cat," Emily said.

"He does that all the time," said Dawn. "He sleeps with me too."

Emily swallowed.

The cat stuck its head in Dawn's neck.

It began to purr.

"He really loves Dawn," said Jill.

"He loves me too," said Emily.

"Me too," said Stacy.

Beast jumped over a crack in the sidewalk. "Let's play giant steps."

"Just a minute," Emily said.

She held up her book. "I have a teeny bit left."

"Just another minute too," Stacy said. "I have to make another *y*."

Emily read the last sentence.

"Terrific," she said.

"You read all that?" Beast asked.

Emily nodded.

"Didn't your eyes get tired?"

"Not one bit."

"Mine don't get tired either," Dawn said.

Stacy put down her paper. "My hand gets tired. Very tired."

"I'll do the calling," Beast said. He stood in the middle of the driveway.

Everyone else went to the end.

"Dawn," Beast called. "You may take two giant steps."

Dawn took two great big giant steps.

Beast started to laugh.

He jumped up and down.

"Go back," he yelled. "You forgot to say 'May I?'"

"You're right." Dawn laughed. She stepped back.

Emily watched Dawn out of the corner of her eye.

The cat was still hanging around Dawn's neck.

Jill was right.

The cat loved Dawn.

Dawn loved the cat too. She was rubbing her chin on its fur.

Too bad, Emily thought. She loved the cat more.

"How many fish do you have?" she asked Dawn.

"I'm not telling," said Dawn.

"Emily," said Beast. "Take two grandma steps."

"May I?"

"Yes, you may," said Beast.

Emily bent over. She took two teeny grandma steps.

She was going to win.

Dawn had only three fish.

She was sure of it.

She tried not to hear the cat purring.

Chapter 10

Emily looked in the mirror.

Her party dress was pink.

It was too short.

Her knees showed. They had two brown scabs.

She made a face.

"Your face looks ugly like that," Stacy said.

Emily felt ugly. She felt like a mongoose.

"What's the matter?" Stacy asked.

Emily didn't answer.

She shook her head.

She kept thinking about the blue fish.

Stacy danced around the bedroom.

She was wearing her party dress too. A yellow one.

"Li-berry par-par-party," Stacy sang. "Will I get my card today?"

"Write small," Emily said. "Write dark."

They went downstairs.

Their mother was in the hall. "You look great," she said.

"Except for my knees," said Emily.

Her mother smiled. "You're growing. The dress is a little short. We'll have to get you a new one after school starts."

Emily and Stacy went down the street.

They waved back at their mother.

They turned in at the library door.

Mrs. Baker was standing at a table. She was giving out juice and cupcakes.

She smiled at them. "I have to ask you something later."

Emily nodded. She said hello to Jill.

Then she went over to the Fish for a Good Book chart.

Dawn was standing there.

Emily looked over her shoulder.

She could see her four fish. Two tan ones, a red one, and that blue one.

She looked at Dawn's name.

Dawn still had only three fish.

She had lost.

Emily could take the cat home.

She took a deep breath.

Stacy danced over to them. She waved a paper around.

"I have to write my name," she said. "Small and dark. Right?"

"Right," Emily said.

She leaned over Stacy. She watched her make the *S*.

She looked at Dawn. Dawn's face was red.

"Where's the cat?" Emily asked.

"He's home." Dawn had tears in her eyes. "On my bed. I told him it was the last time."

"Oh," said Emily. She watched Stacy make the *a*.

"Very nice. Right, Emily?" Stacy asked.

"Yes."

"I worked hard on this," Stacy told Dawn.

"That's good," Dawn said.

"Are you crying?" Stacy asked.

"No," Dawn said.

Stacy finished her name. She went to the front.

Emily looked at the chart again.

Freddie had a bunch of fish. So did Edward.

Beast's sister, Holly, had the most.

Emily looked at her own fish.

She thought about the cat. Maybe he would miss Dawn.

Dawn wasn't a mongoose.

She wasn't a cheater either.

She read big fat books.

Emily reached up.

She dug under the thumbtack. She pulled off the blue fish.

It left a space in the middle of the other fish.

She turned to Dawn. "We both have three fish. We're even Steven."

Dawn's mouth opened. She still had tears in her eyes. "How come?"

"It was a mistake," Emily said. "Someone put it up by mistake."

Dawn wiped at her eyes. "Who gets the cat?"

"We could choose," Emily said slowly.

Stacy came to the back.

She had a blue library card. "I'm going to

get a book," she said. "One with lots of pictures."

"All right," Emily said.

"Do we get the cat?" asked Stacy.

Emily didn't answer for a minute. Then she shook her head. "No. Dawn gets Pickle Puss."

"Powder Puff," said Dawn.

"I think we need a dog anyway," said Stacy. "I'm going to find a book about one."

"You saved my life," Dawn said.

"Let's get some juice," said Emily.

They went over to Mrs. Baker.

"You helped Stacy with her name," Mrs. Baker said. "You're a neat kid."

Dawn squeezed Emily's arm. "You are."

Emily felt wonderful.

She wasn't a mongoose.

"I wanted to ask you," Mrs. Baker began. "I know you like snakes . . ."

"And cats," said Stacy. She had a book under her arm.

"My neighbor is moving," said Mrs. Baker. "She wants someone to take her gerbil."

"That's us," said Stacy.

Emily smiled. "Right."

"I'll bring it tomorrow," said Mrs. Baker.

Emily nodded. She went over to the shelves. She had to get two books.

One about gerbils.

The other one was a fat one. It was the one Freddie had told her about.

She was going to read like crazy all year.

Next summer she'd be able to fish better than anyone.

Travel Fun with the Polk Street Kids on Tour

Join them as they take to the road to see America. Each fun-filled story includes a kid's guide to the city featuring the best attractions, museums, monuments, maps, and more!

Oh Boy, Boston!
The Polk Street Kids on Tour
Patricia Reilly Giff
Illustrated by Blanche Sims

0-440-41365-6

Look Out, Washington, D.C.!
Patricia Reilly Giff
Illustrated by Blanche Sims

0-440-40934-0

Next Stop, New York City!
The Polk Street Kids on Tour
Patricia Reilly Giff
Illustrated by Blanche Sims

0-440-41362-1

Available from Yearling Books